FIVE FLYING PENGUINS

Barbara Barbieri McGrath

Illustrated by Stephanie Fizer Coleman

ini Charlesbridge

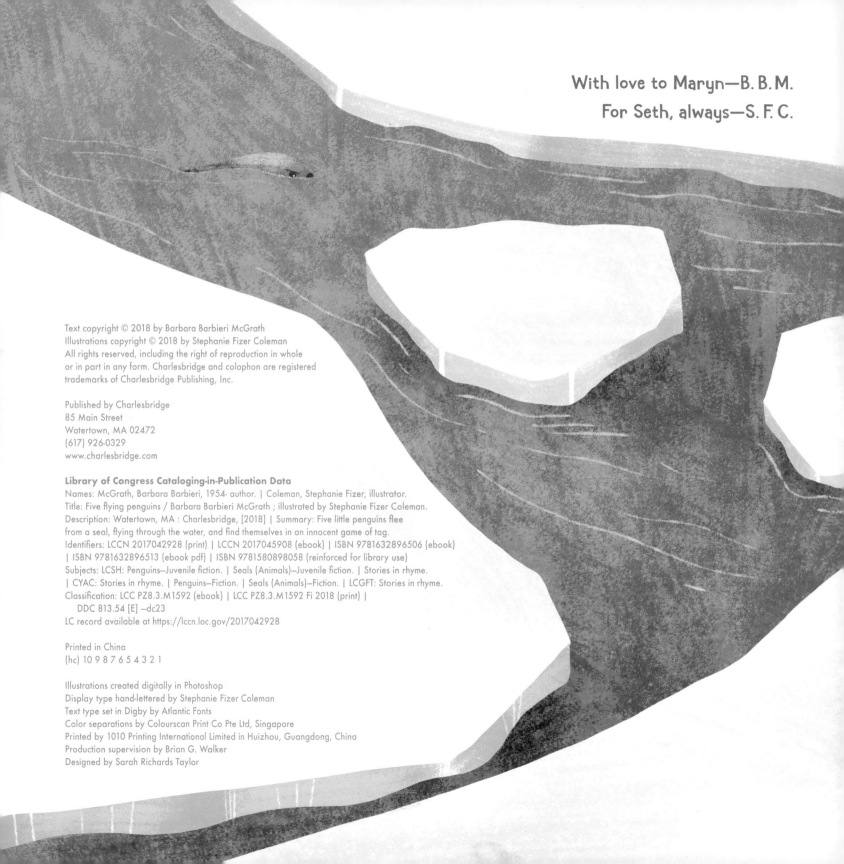

With love to Maryn—B. B. M.
For Seth, always—S. F. C.

Published by Charlesbridge
85 Main Street
Watertown, MA 02472
(617) 926-0329
www.charlesbridge.com

Library of Congress Cataloging-in-Publication Data
Names: McGrath, Barbara Barbieri, 1954- author. | Coleman, Stephanie Fizer, illustrator.
Title: Five flying penguins / Barbara Barbieri McGrath ; illustrated by Stephanie Fizer Coleman.
Description: Watertown, MA : Charlesbridge, [2018] | Summary: Five little penguins flee
from a seal, flying through the water, and find themselves in an innocent game of tag.
Identifiers: LCCN 2017042928 (print) | LCCN 2017045908 (ebook) | ISBN 9781632896506 (ebook)
| ISBN 9781632896513 (ebook pdf) | ISBN 9781580898058 (reinforced for library use)
Subjects: LCSH: Penguins—Juvenile fiction. | Seals (Animals)—Juvenile fiction. | Stories in rhyme.
| CYAC: Stories in rhyme. | Penguins—Fiction. | Seals (Animals)—Fiction. | LCGFT: Stories in rhyme.
Classification: LCC PZ8.3.M1592 (ebook) | LCC PZ8.3.M1592 Fi 2018 (print) |
    DDC 813.54 [E] —dc23
LC record available at https://lccn.loc.gov/2017042928

Printed in China
(hc) 10 9 8 7 6 5 4 3 2 1

Illustrations created digitally in Photoshop
Display type hand-lettered by Stephanie Fizer Coleman
Text type set in Digby by Atlantic Fonts
Color separations by Colourscan Print Co Pte Ltd, Singapore
Printed by 1010 Printing International Limited in Huizhou, Guangdong, China
Production supervision by Brian G. Walker
Designed by Sarah Richards Taylor

Five little penguins,
sitting on the ice . . .

The first one said,

TODAY FEELS VERY nice!

The second one said,

The third one said,

The fourth one said,

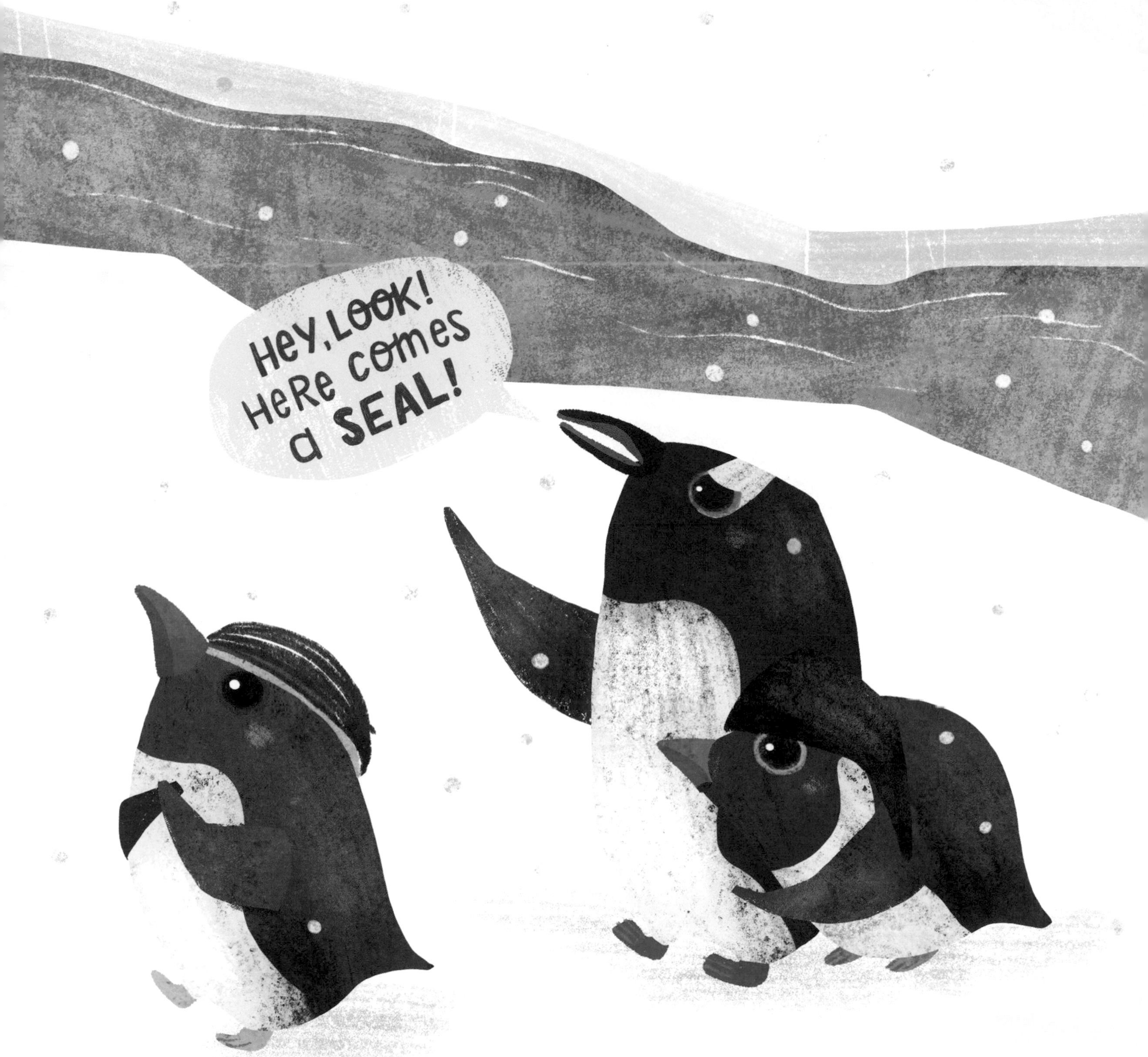
Hey, LOOK! Here comes a SEAL!

PITTER-PATTER

PATTER

went penguin feet,

as they dove right in!

SPL

SASH!

Five flying penguins started
to swim, swim, swim!

FLIP-FLAP

went penguin wings,

as they flew through the sea.

The first one said,

The second one said,

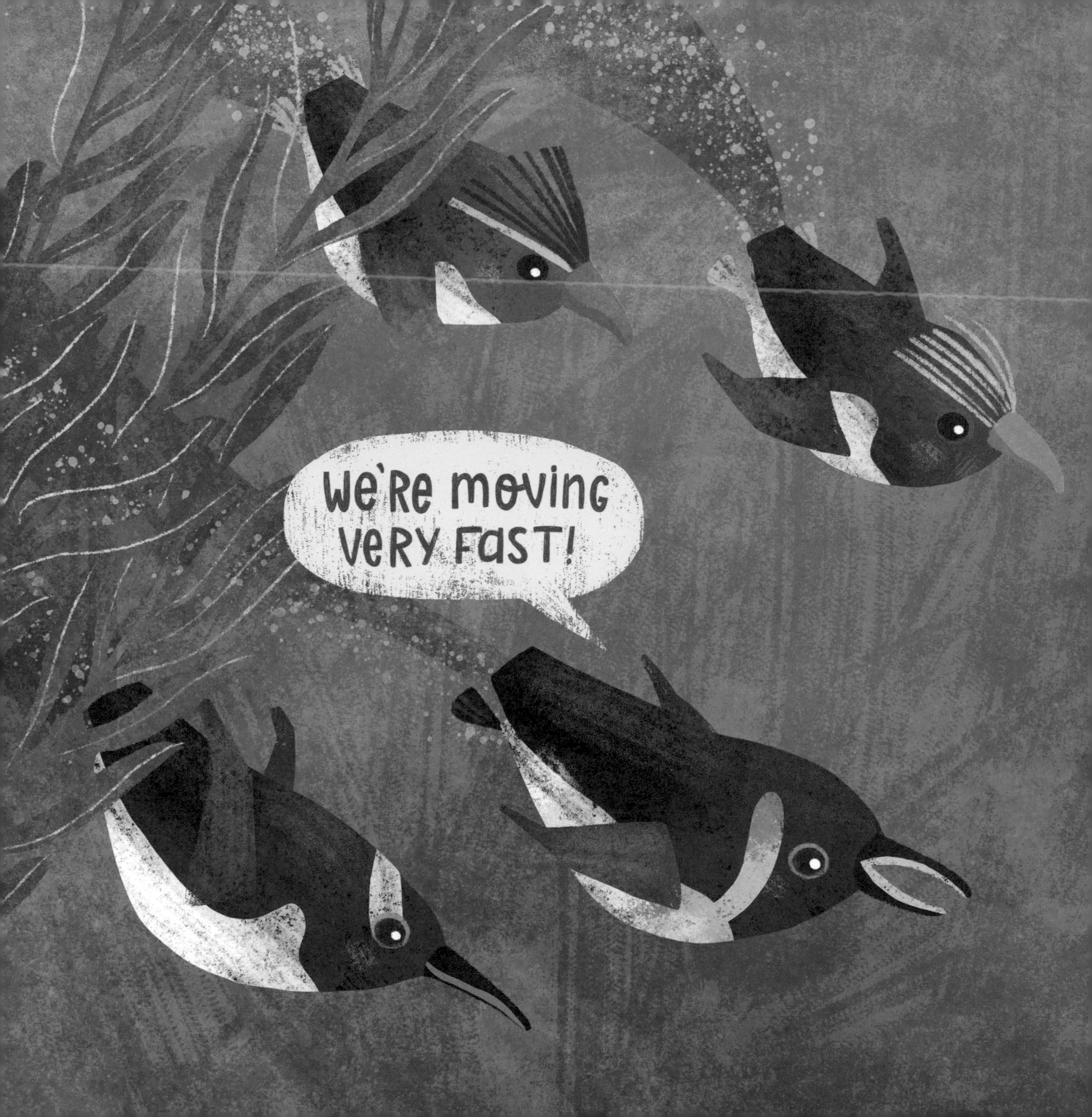
We're moving very fast!

The third one said,

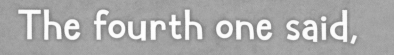
The fourth one said,

The fifth one said,

HONK!

barked the
charging seal.

He just wouldn't quit.

That sneaky, silly seal said,

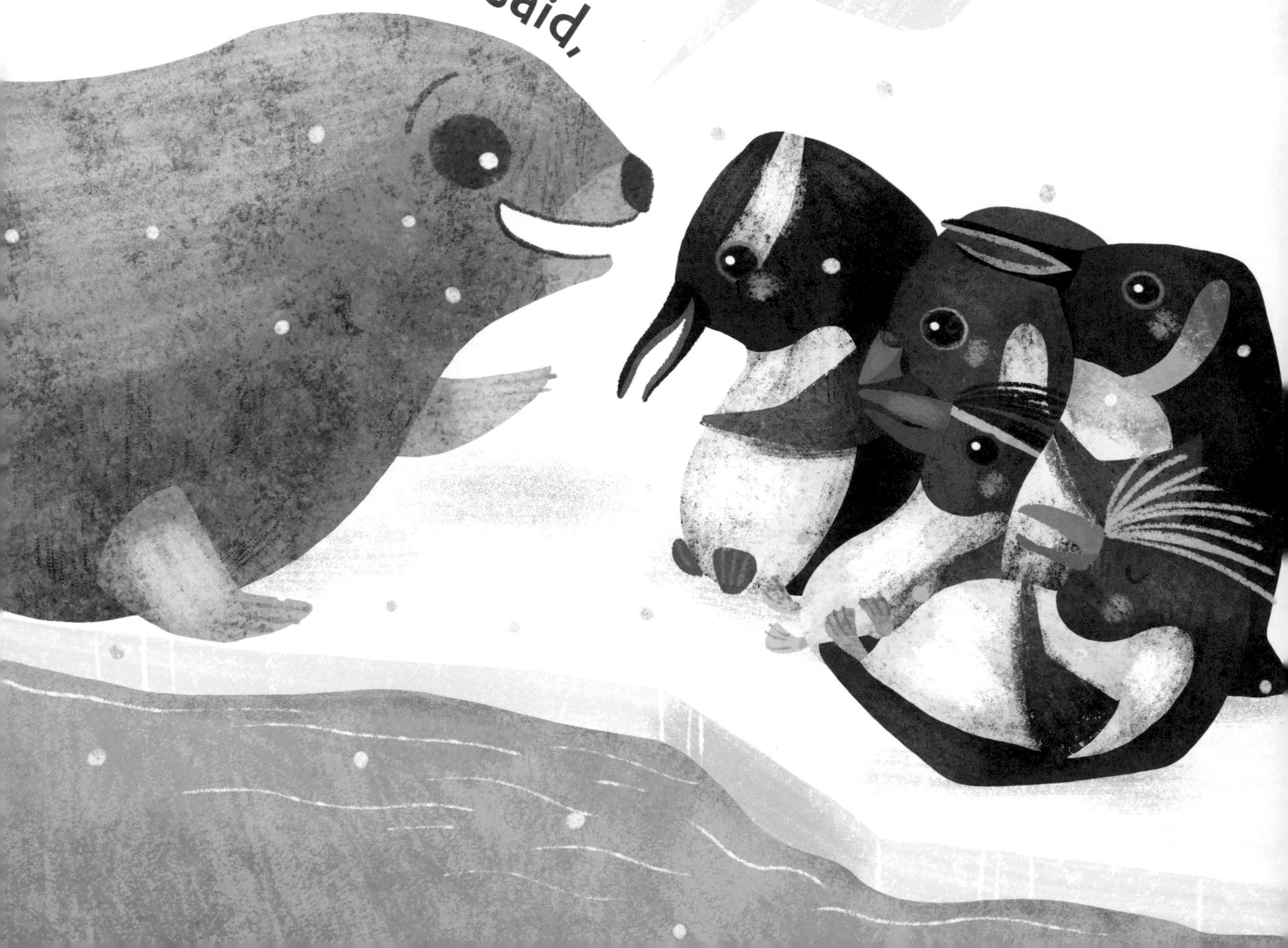